Singing
the
Mozart Requiem

Also by Ingrid Wendt

Moving the House (BOA Editions, 1980)

Singing
the
Mozart Requiem

Ingrid Wendt

Breitenbush Books
Portland, Oregon

First Edition 2 3 4 5 6 7 8 9

Library of Congress Cataloging in Publication Data

Wendt, Ingrid, 1944-
   Singing the Mozart requiem.

I. Title
PS3573.E516S55 1987   811.54   87-5133

ISBN 0-932576-51-6
ISBN 0-932576-52-4 (pbk.)

Publication of this book is made possible, in part, by a grant from the National Endowment for the Arts, a federal agency, to whom the author and publisher express their sincere gratitude.

The author and publisher express their appreciation to the Oregon Arts Commission for a grant that aided in the publication of this book.

The author is also grateful to the University of New Mexico, whose D. H. Lawrence Fellowship provided the time and solitude in which many of these poems were written or begun.

Breitenbush Books are published for James Anderson by Breitenbush
   Publications, P.O. Box 02137, Portland, Oregon 97202.
Patrick Ames, Editor-in-Chief.
Design by: Susan Applegate of Publishers Book Works, Inc.
Cover illustration of a choir stall in the cathedral of Ulm, West Germany, by
   Debbie Berrow
Composition by Irish Setter
Manufactured in U.S.A.

Acknowledgments

Grateful acknowledgment is made to editors and publishers of the following publications in which these poems first appeared:

The Amicus Journal: "Stone"
Backbone 4 (Seal Press): "Fir Tip Jelly"
Backbone: A Journal of Women's Literature: "Fir Tip Jelly"
California Quarterly: "Mussels"
Calliope: "California Interstate 5: Some Travelers' Warnings"
The Chariton Review: "Inflorescence"
Crosscurrents: "Learning the Silence"
Gilt Edge, New Series: "The Willow in Jackson, Wyoming"
Hardscrabble: "Dream"
KSOR GUIDE to the Arts: "In the Teton National Forest," "The House on Douglas Street: A Map," "9:55 P.M.," "*Déjà Vu*"
The Menomonie Review: "No. 14. Duet"
Northwest Magazine (Oregonian): "Kurpark, Bad Homburg"
Poetry Northwest: "Endangered Species"
Poetry Now: "Delicacies"
San José Studies: "Pilgrim Pumpkin"
Sing, Heavenly Muse! Women's Poetry and Prose: "A Bib for Anne's Daughter"

"Singing the Mozart Requiem" first appeared in *Calyx, A Journal of Art and Literature by Women*, Volume 8, Number 3
"Cinderella Dream at Ten" first appeared in *Calyx, A Journal of Art and Literature by Women*, Volume 1, Number 1
"Middle Sister Poem" first appeared as *Poet and Critic* Broadside #1
"Sestina" first appeared in *Poetry*, June 1984
"Another Dream" first appeared in *Swift Kick*, Number 1

This book is dedicated to

Ralph Salisbury, my husband
Erin Salisbury, my daughter
Kathleen Wendt Sikelianos, my sister
and to
The Eugene Concert Choir

For all of the songs given
each of us yet to sing

Contents

III. SINGING THE MOZART REQUIEM

"What is past is not dead;
it is not even past.
We cut ourselves off from it;
we pretend to be strangers."

Christa Wolf
A Model Childhood

(Translated by Ursule Molinaro
and Hedwig Rappolt)

I

ENDANGERED SPECIES

Endangered Species

If I had been five minutes later, or ten,
earlier, or hadn't gone down the lane for mail, the fields
of alfalfa ripe with robins, a fresh crop of grasshoppers

If the coyote flashing through one chance lift
of my head from a book, in broad daylight, hadn't
gone the wrong way, detoured by one rabbit less

Or the bear whose track I found on my way back
fresh and unmistakable as a blinking red light,
had staked out in just the right place, I might

Never have seen the pause of wild turkeys under
the shelter of pines: aloof, the eternal
black robes of mourning; steady as county fair targets

One by one leisurely along
the edge of the field, the creek, up the hill into trees,
the edge of extinction, beyond

All powers of observation. Purposeful.
As if there were others to take their place.
As if all of us had all the time in the world.

Mussels

for Ralph

We've learned where the big ones grow,
to harvest not from the tops of rocks where shells
fill with sand

to follow the tide out to the farthest reefs we can reach
and still not get wet, where last time we found
giant anemones green-sheathed and dripping under

the overhangs like the cocks of horses, we laughed, or
elephants, having each come to the same conclusion,
fresh from bed and married long enough

to say such things to each other, again
to remember the summer we first discovered mussels
big as fists protecting Sisters Rocks.

Just married and ready for anything, even
mussels were game, black as obsidian, stubbornly
clinging to rocks, to each other, their shells

so tightly together we had to force them apart
with a knife, the meat
inside a leap of orange, poppy-bright; and when

three perch in a row took the hook you'd baited
tender as liver we said we must try them ourselves
someday, if they're safe, which they weren't

all the years we lived down south: red algae in summer
tides infiltrating our chance to experiment, food without precedent,
how would we know what to do?

Counting at last on friends who had been to Europe and now
are divorced, we waded waist deep to pick some,
scraping our knuckles raw on barnacles

none of us knowing to soak our catch two hours at least
to clean out the sand; the sand we took in with butter and lemon
cleaning our teeth for a week.

Now we can't get our fill of them.
Weekend vacations you work to the last, cooking
one more batch to freeze for fritters or stew.

Now we harvest them easily, take the right tools, wear boots
we gave to each other for birthdays so we don't have
to remember to watch out for waves

to feel barnacles unavoidably crushed underfoot
like graveyards of dentures waves have exposed, although
sometimes now I find myself

passing over the biggest, maybe because
they've already survived the reach of starfish,
blindly prowling on thousands of white-tipped canes,

or they've grown extra barnacles,
limpets, snails, baby anemones,
rock crabs hiding behind. As though

age after all counts for something
and I've grown more tender-hearted,
wanting you not to know about the cluster

I found today, for the first
time in years having taken time off from job
and housework and child care, sleeping so late

my feet got wet on the incoming tide, unexpectedly
talking aloud, saying look at that one, bigger even
than Sisters Rocks: a kind of language

marriage encourages, private as memories of mussels,
anachronistic as finding I miss you
picking mussels to take home to you

not the ones you'd pick if you could but fresh
as any young lover's bouquet and far more edible,
more than enough to last us at least a week.

Sestina

for Rich

The day you found him started
like any other vacation, the children
awake ahead of the best part of your final
dream, the sun like a thin arm
plucking the tips of waves like feathers, a race against
rain, high tide, no time

for breakfast. This time
no one started
without you, nothing was against
your will. When the children
worried over the starfish missing an arm
you could tell them nothing was final,

as if you had the final
say and time
was on your side, an arm
you'd only started
to raise between the children
and what you were up against.

Finding him there against
the base of the cliff like the final
opinion you hadn't planned on, the children
knew he wasn't asleep, but for a time
you tried not to believe them, you started
to shake his arm

as if in waking him you could arm
yourself against
words of three doctors, the cancer started
too early to tell how final
this time
on the beach with the children,

next week's operation, the children
told more than you knew you could say. Arm
under his head, no time
to explain, against
knowledge forcing a final
breath into his lungs, what started

there started without you: the children
a final time saying they knew all along he was dead; at arm's
length, untouchable, this fact against all you'd yet say, given time.

6

Pictures, South of Seal Rock

1

Ruby Johnson, who tosses the seagulls and one crow
table scraps out of a pail, blames
the dredge in Newport Bay for the sand.

There aren't enough clams, she says, for her birds.
They need her, orbit around her sun-yellow slicker
each morning before she raises a hand.

Where she stands was thirty years ago nothing
but rock, a shelf
edging up to the cliff:

red, gold, orange, brown exposed
by rain and swirled smooth as shells,
toboggan runs, canyons at

Zabriski Point, whose colors
in sun not even the films of Antonioni
could catch.

2

And farther south, where these rocks end,
clams once were so thick Ruby could get
her limit without
trying, her husband
always got fish.

Today she says it takes longer, which may
be why all
we ever get each time is wet
up to our waists, our sleeves
full of sand to the elbows, never

finding the hole like a tiny volcano
sucking back its own eruption
each time a wave shuttles in still
more sand from the north, or so
the science film said: a natural

pattern we saw in slow
motion—red
dye relentless as lava, out and in

7

and down, the trail of a headless fowl.
That's how, they said, harbors fill.

3

In winter even the tidepools are full.
I remember last summer the way anemones
blazed under water like meteors
all in a row: balls of green fire,

as they entered our atmosphere, caught
on film, each frame a slight
variation on what came before, how
I tried to make everything stop!

My camera went where I went, and I mourned
double exposures, a roll I shot and later found
the winding spool never
took up. Oh,

I wanted forever to see again pea crabs
I mistook for pebbles until a shadow
chased them away
and tidepools

so complex it took more
patience than focus to find
occasional snails
orange as mussel meat,

hermit crabs, starfish, chitons, all
covered in winter with sand so deep
we walked over the rocks as over soft
shoulders, anemones popping like blisters,

my trust in a natural balance framed
by assumptions only a newcomer makes,
the sun for weeks at a time in clouds
so thick I swore it would never return.

Fir Tip Jelly

In spring, when the tips of each branch bristle
green as sunlight wrapped into the crests of waves
and you for once have remembered to bring
ladder and boots for climbing, are wearing

a shirt that can take permanent sap, you don't mind
vacation time you can't spend on the beach, for hours
hair filling with needles and bark,
steam in your kitchen clouding the windows,

pot liquor gray as the months ahead when no one will
notice, fir tip or Welch's, what's
on peanut butter.
No matter. You're making what one day

you saw at the county fair and swore
someday you'd try. And some other day
you'll pick, like the pioneers did, kinnikinnick,
twinberry, salmonberry, wild lily of the valley, already

around your ladder more salal blossoms than dates in history:
rows of small white bells balanced
on last year's growth like time lines you'll never get straight
or catch up on, uncovering secrets the Forest Service

preserves, recipes
next to drawings of leaves thin as the difference between
Douglas fir and Sitka spruce, which
if you haven't already checked with the guide you could have

picked by mistake (and may
or may not be poison).
County Extension says
if this happens, to spray it on

bugs in your garden, although there's no way
(since it's after all spring and nothing is
even planted) to keep
scum thick as oatmeal from bubbling under the lid

or to know in advance these processes
history doesn't record: trials

and errors of good intentions even
pioneers must have made, somehow

sometimes succeeding without your clear advantage:
food coloring which, not knowing yet how
little good it will do, green as springtime you
trust will do the trick.

Mushroom Picking, I Talk With a Bear

*"Whenever I feel afraid, I hold my head erect,
and whistle a happy tune, and no one will suspect
I'm afraid."*

Oscar Hammerstein
The King and I

I could of course moralize, say forgetting to sing
was what did it. Or haste, one last chance:
chanterelles blunt tongues dissolving luminous
into the too-early dusk, unrecognizable
constellations ready to wink and go out. Oh,

I knew what I was after, climbing alone on the overgrown
logging road, wading the inarticulate grass
snarled brown. And maybe the bear did, too: that
unmistakable scat I stepped around
fresh with the orchard just that morning I'd been

told was raided, telling me if I wanted to keep
going I'd have to belt out a human announcement,
keep it up through clouds closing darker than moss
around me, thick glisten of needles, the edges
of leaves and air between blurring. And yes,

the bear would have been there anyway, I might
never have known: focusing not on the words
I was singing, no Anna lost in Siam, and I wasn't
afraid, though maybe I should have been,
thinking instead of someone I should have

long before this forgotten, last words
that never were spoken: hidden
months, years at a time, deep as mycelium
feeding on decay this possible danger I couldn't
identify. No field guide for it. Nothing to see.

No excuse, that day in the Coast Range forgetting
to sing, at last the mushrooms I hunted for opening
out of the gloom: golden
wings, victory
marking the edge of the road. No

mistaking that low unambiguous roar,
my surprise at how close

anything big as that could not be heard coming
"Bear," I said, loud as I could. "I hear you.
Don't worry. I'm here. You're there. That's fine."

Bear language I made up on the spot,
trusting what mattered was not
what I said but that I was saying it, no
question at all of running away from it,
silent as humus my fingers

picking double time more than I'd come for:
chanterelles, fir needles, soil
still in the making; wordless
resolve I took with the dinner
down the hill. The basis for

moral decision a moment's experience shifts.
Behind me, a bear
too real to be a metaphor.
Somewhere ahead, the letter
I didn't yet know I would write.

Middle Sister Poem

Real as the ridge
line children draw sharp on the edge
of mountains, there's a point

friendship sometimes will reach,
thin as a footstep between
east and west, where one of you

won't go on and the wind
to the other says *Don't look
back or you're gone*.

Up ahead, the peak
you can climb
alone. And then?

California Interstate 5: Some Travelers' Warnings

Silent as the false
teeth we found in the rest
stop restroom halfway between
Ball's Ferry and Jelly's Ferry roads

silent as Fourth of July all summer
bursts of oleander lining
the freeway   profusion of fuchsia
magenta   crimson   cushioning
north from southbound traffic

the fact of their poison

my mother's friend's story
of soldiers on leave from
the war   who never
returned   having chosen a twig
to stir their coffee
instead of a spoon

messages I
wouldn't hear anyway

car Japanese-made and purring
content as a lion at thirty-five miles
per gallon past a plague of oil wells
grasshopper heads single-
mindedly drinking their fill

trusting as red-winged blackbirds
perched on cattails deep in the ditch
or the chicken shiny as bootblack
scratching shoulder gravel miles
from any farm

determined
as giant crows   one
every few miles   flapping
off the attacks of sparrows

or
the biplane dusting fields for medfly
shooting up over the highway
after each row like a killer
whale in a show   so low
over the road its shadow
could swallow us all.

14

The Willow in Jackson, Wyoming

1

Someone wanted to save it, pruned it
high as car tops, judged the line
between asphalt and roots thin as a dare

the limit sentiment could stretch
across our balcony view of Cache and Pearl,
gift shops, museum, the scene

of the evening shoot-out, the loser always
living for ski season, mountains stockaded
dead-end of every street in Jackson.

2

Out of the context of neon, the Hitching Post Tavern, a time
when holiday lights were once a year
and the transformation of branches to sky was more

delicate even than these
constellations of miniature bulbs
whorled around branches too many to see,

their wire connections invisible as the flight of Pegasus,
threat of The Bear, that incomprehensible pitcher spilling
all of the Milky Way.

3

White as the piles of linen
the driver delivered, the truck
at two in morning at getaway speed shot

everyone out of sleep,
leaves from the branches, the trunk
of the tree back down to its first six years.

The rain of glass the sound
of all most gentle
small promises breaking.

In the Teton National Forest

Porcupines, hungry as spring
for freshness, young tips of trees
or else it could have been lightning
I said, one snap judgement
of clouds lower
than a squirrel is safe.

But the seedling at home, transplanted from
the base of our friends' own tree
is split at the top like the rest, you said.

And then we found one other trunk
divided not two but three
parallel ways: a quiver
of arrows, rifles
held at attention,
rockets years beyond us.

Learning the Silence

*"When Japanese arrange flowers, the space
between the flowers is considered,
the shape of space between."*

Ellen Bass

You've been here before, your ears insist,
though you know it's not true,
there's nothing to count on—no vague

perk of the coffee pot, faraway
lawnmowers measuring tolerance—
how much space between small irritations

you used to call *quiet*
consoling as traffic
vibrations rocking the cells of sleep.

Alert as zinnias, sea anemones
poised for the least touch, here
in this cabin remote on this mountain

your ears put out feelers, any
moment a message, your ears
hollow as shells are on call:

Pine cone on roof!
Hummingbird's wings!
Nuthatch checking the bark for bugs!

And what comes in between:
silence
so sure of itself

nothing you do can
ignore it, escape it.
Whatever sound is next is yours.

Learning the Clouds

"Rain crows can't be trusted up here.
None of the signs up here can be trusted."

Al Bearce, Manager
D. H. Lawrence Ranch, New Mexico

If this were Oregon under such sky, each day
it would rain. Morning clouds scouting
the western horizon bringing back more would know
what to do with themselves,
when it was time to quit grouping and re-
grouping like hands of cards covering all bets until
someone somewhere else lays down first and all

is waste: cloud the orchard could have used,
this one for cattle nuzzling sand,
one for this mountain whose air is so dry my
thoughts of home spark static between them,
so thin when my stomach growls the sound
startles the horse in the meadow below.

Knocking on wood I say so far I'm lucky,
Gallina Creek isn't quite dry. I wait
all day to wash dishes, all week to bathe.
The water I used to let run while brushing my teeth
I shut off between rinses, the toilet
unflushed until odor insists: simple

rituals no one is witness to,
nothing like carrying water up ladders in pueblos
or hauling whole tankfuls to cabins in trucks.
Nothing sacred as corn dances
tourists cluster around like beads
on rosaries, circle suspecting something here

must be understood: *Zia*
the sun-shaped capitol building in Santa Fe
imitates: sun
around which all life in this land
revolves, the clouds
just passing by I try

as though it were the least I could do, to name:

Cirrostratus   Cumulonimbus   Stratocumulus
Cirrus   Stratus   Cumulus   Nimbus
Cumulus   Cumulus   Cumulus.

El Santuario de Chimayo

1

They are all here, as always parked in
whatever shade is left: Winnebago *La Familia
Ruiz*, pickups, imports, Greyhound
charter bus. Children
inside the courtyard, around

and around the tombstones. Grandmothers
in whom all the sorrow
again is only beginning, waiting.
Those who have come from inside.
Those gathering strength to go in.

Dust from the parking lot shuffling sun,
settling, unobserved: feet
of miracles too tiny to claim.
Across the street: hamburgers, hot dogs, tamales.
Film in the Potrero Trading Post nearly always all gone.

2

Dim, the fidget of votive
candles, spotlight on
the altar, gilded *retablos*

carved almost two hundred years ago
fresh as silk
roses, carnations, handmade

lace on the altarcloth. Here
no one speaks, no one smiles,
all attention

ahead on the crucifix. Lips
fluttering: petals,
bouquet in the breath of God. Paid for,

trailing, knee by knee all the way up
the aisle, silent as hem stitches, whatever sins
this one woman could own.

3

Miracles happen here: *milagros*
like afternoon thunderstorms in the Sangre
de Cristos, predictable, who
knows on whom they will fall?

Earth from the back room—the hole, always
almost full, where once a mysterious icon
hundreds of miles from its absence
was found—this

same earth, eaten or even
touched, has made the lame
walk, the blind
see: mute

display on the walls, the proof, footsteps
of legend: rows of
crutches, remnants of dis-
belief, left behind.

4

Miracles yet
to come, leaving nothing to chance, for love of
someone back home

these Dixie cups, plastic bags, envelopes, here
the faithful take turns,
the earth they have come for obligingly powdered.

Sand. "Stand in it. Stand in it. Go
on!" this mother orders her son. "Both
feet! Step down!" This halo

over his head, his neck, his shoulders,
dust she fusses into his shirt: the miracle
set to begin.

Old man on the bench. Like bars of a crib
the walker holding him back. "Here,
Grandpa," the girl

says. "Dirt. Dirt."
"*¿Tierra?*"
"Dirt."

5

Please Dear God help my husband control his drinking
smoking and to become a part of you Keep us in your prayers

Corners of envelopes, lined
paper from memo books, backs of deposit slips, these
messages edged into picture frames,

garlands of hope
grounded, public
the seeds of despair.

"Prayers," someone whispers.
"This place is improved," the man with her says.
"Last time, there wasn't this kind of floor."

6

Front of the Potrero Trading Post—overhang
dripping with *ristras*, red hot souvenir chiles
like so many teeth; delinquent
the horns of bulls, shriveled

in sun—the owners' children argue
over the bicycle: whose
turn. Dust
scowling their feet.

Silent,
alone in the bank
of cottonwoods, over
and over the youngest

funneling
sand, one hand
to the back of the other,
ghost-thin the powder he washes

each time off in the creek,
returning, his own
hourglass
good for a whole afternoon.

Squash Blossom Necklace:
Millicent Rogers Museum, Taos, N.M.

Granada (*Sp.*): 1. Province of southern Spain. 2. The capital
of Granada in the central part of the province; site of
the Alhambra, the palace built in the thirteenth and
fourteenth centuries for Moorish kings. 3. Pomegranate.
4. Hand-grenade.

Silver descendant
of Moorish tradition Spain
absorbed like hail—turned into rain—all over

Granada sprouting
the glittering *naja*—fertile, the crescent
moon inverted: good

luck spilling like stars,
the fate of the Navajo for whom the moon
like a serpent

twined between this world and that
below, slender
as vines, bringing

news—squash
blossoms that centuries later in silver
would echo, hollow as bells

another defeat—transmuted through Mexico,
flowers of the *granada* in Navajo
hands flourishing

where farmlands were taken,
New Mexico desert
once fertile with miles of

irrigation—all attention
as far back as memory can go, channeled in
self-defense, towards war.

Pilgrim Pumpkin

> 25¢
> Connecticut Field
> (*Cucurbita Pepo*)

said the Northrup King display
in the University Bookstore that when I
was in school was the co-op

> Grow pumpkins like the Pilgrims did.
> Plant a little history
> in your own back yard.

A pumpkin different, you think, from
all others, some purer strain, direct
descendant from the *May-*
flower, but no!

> The pumpkin has been around longer
> than you think. At least
> 7,000 years. Archeologists have found
> pieces of pumpkin rind in the ancient ruins of
> the Cliff Dwellers and Basket Weavers
> in the southwestern United
> States.

That other pumpkin we picked from the middle
of our own lot the morning our house
moved in

That pumpkin had a history too:
seed a single survivor of tilling, vacant lot
weeds once the garden of Robert Keefe

who built for his mother-in-law the house next door
whose plans were drawn for his own
who planted the apple tree
I built my daughter's sandbox under
over the spot where later
I learned the old lady's heart
stopped

whose widow who sold us this lot now lives next door alone

That pumpkin whose seeds we saved for next year's garden
coming from not
just one but thousands
of previous pumpkins

> Which certainly qualifies
> the pumpkin as a true
> native American

Chromosomes linked like arrows: arm in arm in
arms: truths innocent
of good as of harm

of words of pride
of a nation
a father, a mother

My daughter, Hallowe'en Sunday child chanting

> "My great great
> great great grand-
> mother was
> an Indian
> woo-woo-woo-woo-woo"

The child I was in grade school boasting "I

> am one hundred percent
> German"

because everyone else was already
melted in the pot
my name was Ingrid which made me
special, my father
Chilean (but German)
my mother from Michigan (German)

The child not knowing Germany had
just lost another war, not knowing
what war was
that her parents refused
to teach her German for fear of what people would think

Her father refusing to fight, his heart
tolling in her like a bell, a *copihue*

blood-red Chilean
national flower growing high
on its vine, the song
she—barely a woman—learned, tracing
backwards steps he took away forever, the song
she learned to play
on his brother's borrowed guitar

> *"Aquí mismito te dejo*
> *hecho un copihue mi corazón"*

The child the woman she was
trying to keep
alive in Villa Alemana, calling
through every market for
a pumpkin
> *"Calabaza, calabaza"*

the word the dictionary said
> *"Calabaza"*

not gourd
> *"Calabaza"*

not squash

Pumpkin, there!

> *"¡Ay!*
> *¡Cidracayote!"*

Pumpkin
meat solid to the core

I
the child the woman
my small college sent to bear goodwill
and understanding, bearing the need
to explain away Goldwater, Johnson, Viet-
nam beginning, to mourn a Kennedy I barely knew

Mississippi summer
How any grown nation could hate
so much

Explaining instead a pumpkin hollowed out
for Hallowe'en, a jack-o'-lantern
that after so much effort must
be good for something

Myth I invent
because a myth is needed

Procession of cousins behind a grinning pumpkin face
we carry like the Child of God, Mexican children's
candles winding through dark streets
The Legend of Sleepy Hollow

> *"Lo mismo cómo hacemos*
> *en los Estados Unidos"*

I
being borne next morning to graves
of grandmother, grandfather, everyone
in town with flowers (buying), flowers (selling), All
Saints' Day mass pilgrimage in which my own
grows silent as a seed

Nothing
is that simple any more.

> Consider this: pump-
> kin vines may be
> trained to climb a trel-
> lis or fence. This takes
> less space and can
> give an exceedingly
> handsome effect. The
> fruit will hang safely.

That pumpkin we saved from the new
foundation of our house

Pumpkin whose seeds saved for next year's garden grew
their vines between a dozen other vines, a summer-
fall-winter-squash harvest
grew

other seeds
whose genes like the souls of pollen

bees run
together like paint:

turban-pumpkin
Danish pumpkin, yellow crookneck-
pumpkin, butternut, zucchini, patty-
pan-pumpkin

next year's indefinite orange and green.

Kurpark, Bad Homburg

Here, where often the Kaiser came from Berlin
hundreds of miles by train, his own private station
now a nightclub, the gambling casino
Dostoyevsky is said to have lost and kept on losing in,
still the same glamorous destination here at the end of
park benches pacing the distance
fountain to fountain where still the elderly stroll:

this water good for the heart, for digestion;
taste aside, this one good for the joints;
this one named for Elizabeth Brunnen, whoever
she was today majestic in stone overlooking
this garden of tulips, magnolias, this not-
so-young-herself American woman
jogging, she tells herself, for all the years

still between herself and these elegant pensioners—
arm in arm, in groups, who have already been through one,
at least, maybe two wars she cannot begin to imagine—
amazed at this woman running from something all of us
too well foresee. Around the next corner, this frog
splashing in stone, the golden ball in his hands in the pond
shiny as promise: that one kiss, which of us ever forgets.

Gast im Schloss

Upstairs in this castle, the same
romance of armor: swords, shields,
halberds each with the same

half-moon axe polished, the opposite iron
claw someone somewhere was killed with or
meant to be: empty

this chain mail someone somewhere else forged
link by link by the thousands by hand. And
on these helmets once measured to fit

the style of each artist, unique,
chromosome-thin, each engraving a glorious proliferation
of flowers and leaves, medallions, classical

heroes, their own
elaborate hearts long before Shakespeare
thought of it etched on their sleeves,

the hilt of this sword handle: lovers reclining
as once in this same chamber there must have been moments
no one gave thought to what this stone castle was for.

Stone

Small as a molar, wisdom tooth
smooth and rootless, wild
rose color milky as taffy, this

delicate stone I find in the gravel
I bless, hold to the light, a treasure out
of filler material dirt depends on, becoming a road,

having already blessed each day without thinking of road
builders, for weeks my solitude deep
in the side of the Sangre de Cristos so complete

coyotes in broad daylight visit my meadow,
eagles roost unalarmed above. Territorial, only
the rufous hummingbird somehow I thought I should feed.

I never thought about gravel: where
it must come from—the side of some other mountain
gawking forever where once there was only a yawn.

Yaquina Head, back home, where once a year murre,
proper as penguins, relinquish the waves to nest.
Rock the bill in Washington last spring failed to save.

Stone I hold in my hand, place on my bookshelf,
light, the color of dawn, the end
of some other solitude, once more traveling on.

After a Strong Wind

Other
sound return
slowly, the way
the first
star blink on
unannounced.

Horses snuffling
weeds in the meadow.
Warbler patching the thicket
with song.
Flies on the screen
desperate again to get in.

See? See? Invisible
in the scrub oaks below,
western flycatcher clearing
the air before landing, again
and again the single
note like a spear: See?

Like thoughts catching up to you.
Things you have known
all along.

II

A SHELTER OF DOLLS

A Shelter of Dolls

Perhaps it began with the ornaments—fabric scraps
turned into mushrooms and teddy bears, flowers, birds, felt
storybook characters accurate down to the last
extra half-hour. You never saw such a tree. Or generosity,
how they would go to relatives, friends, neighbors just
over for coffee. Casual. As though right then
nothing else mattered. As though
this one didn't take more than a day to make,
production line in her living room all year long.

Or earlier, purpose like security going
before four children were grown—or nearly, two
still at home when their step-father isn't
fighting with them (his own, she says, lie and steal), or they
aren't fighting their real father, thrown out of school—
their pictures in oils in the living room, forever small.

It's nobody's fault, she says, they're good kids,
they help with charities, Children's Services, church
bazaars she's always in charge of—all summer, rummage sale
items in her garage, collecting like Saturday re-runs,
some things don't change all at once.
The youngest has all the boys after her.

Myself, I remember an answer from church camp.
Thirteen, I asked why people grew up. To have
children, our group leader said, so they some day can have
their own children. All he left out
curing tomorrow like salt, the girl on the label
spilling it, each time smaller, her picture
within a picture within her own hands
smaller, smaller, smaller.

The House on Douglas Street: A Map

Here is the house on Douglas Street

Here is the willow they planted in back of the neighbors
behind the house on Douglas Street

Here is the pear tree the father once picked
the bat in; the apple, too small for climbing;
fruit too wormy for eating; in front of the willow
behind the house on Douglas Street

Here, the two other apples, hammock between—tempting
the children to alley-oop-over, pulling the rope
all the way to concussion—the mother, pregnant,
thinking she held death in her arms, green
as the apples, the pear, the willow she wasn't right then
aware of behind the house on Douglas Street

Here is the cherry, no branches for climbing, looming
over the playhouse, the mint in the garden, petunias,
the blanket after supper spread on the grass, the father
ready to catch the girl—each time on the ladder higher,
higher than the apple, the pear, the willow, small
below, behind the house on Douglas Street

And the plums no one ate—no one
but the wheels of the car picked up—
they don't count

And the apples in front the girl picked up
for 10¢ a bushel, the honor of helping—smashed,
wormy, too close to grave conclusions—they
don't count

But oh, the cherry south of her window,
its branches the squirrel—not knowing she watched—
came close in; cherry the rope swing hung in;
cherry Barbara fell out of;

here, the cherry she'd eat in all afternoon:
around her, for her, fruit
endless as morning cartoons;

trees outside her second-floor window in spring
she couldn't see through, blossoms becoming
clouds the Baltimore oriole built a nest in, sunset

flashing all childhood long, all
around the house on Douglas Street.

Cinderella Dream at Ten

Each night under the tree the same wolf
waits for The Beauty to fall
down into the gravel circle the children
draw each day for marbles
            (gravel fine as salt: ground
              into your knees it has to
              work itself out)

Each night the same wolf waits and no one
else is there to save
The Beauty waiting alone inside her

flowing yellow hair, the wolf snapping at her
plain blue skirts draped gracefully
over the lowest branch
            (skirts the mice her only real
              friends will trim with ribbons, lace, scraps
              her wicked step-sisters don't need)

So there's no question: each night
you in your father's car
            (your father driving)

drive past the playground, your heart
in your knees even before
you see her
            (in the tree where she always is)

struggle open the door,
struggle her into the seat beside you,
struggle to slam the door on the wolf who is
already gobbling down
            (as you knew he would, painlessly)

your own legs
from toes to knees

waking you
right at the hemline of your own short skirt

knowing it's happened before, your toes are
still there, not to cry out, knowing it's after

all the price you pay for Beauty.

Against Regret

"Love you," my sister says always last
second before we hang up, and you've
heard it, too, maybe said it
offhand as a habit, and said it
knowing it has to sound that way or it won't

work: like dates you mother and father for years
put on the bottom of birthday cards, meaning
this is for keeping, this is to be saved, and God
knows you've tried, a clutter of good
intentions, charms against regret by now scattered

who knows where: the child
you almost remember each night in the inescapable dark
blessing like beads on a rosary each last
star bright name she can think of. Responsible.
Up to her not to leave anyone out.

The Teacher I Wanted to Be

my own forever, my mother
asked home to lunch each spring,

each spring someone new:
Miss Bloss, Mrs. Kuk, Miss Michaelson never
suspecting we waited for blossom time,

hoping the rain would hold off long enough,
counting the days like notes of that year's recital piece
always I played for her, practising

hours longer than any
hundred years' sleep any child could ever imagine:
the princess, the castle awakening, parting

branches blossoming over that aisle of tulips and lilacs, bright
promises I didn't know I was making someday
to become that same teacher each spring

on the last day of school surprised by a girl planting
instead of a secret next to the ear bent low
a kiss, so quick she never could hear what running

all the way home, crying, she all year
had listened for: yes, she was
yes, a good girl

a good
girl
a good girl.

On the Nature of Tact

Poor teacher, her new dress is ugly, the girl
sees clearly: polka dots, hundreds
of little white lies exposed

on black nylon, obvious as
the permanent smell she has
nowhere to hide from, who

will sit next to her? How could her mother
force on her curls like notebook
spirals, blackboard-stiff, her dignity

shorter by three
inches at least. How
could the teacher believe her own words

confidential as grade books, bending
close, "Why dear, your hair looks so nice."
"Thank you, Miss Erickson. That's a pretty new dress."

9:55 P.M.

Alone in the kitchen, this table
made from a door, cleared of everything
but paper, pencil, plants.

On windowsills other plants
double in darkness,
their breath that in the morning
in the steam of coffee making will porthole
this glass like my daughter's eager nose,

tonight self-effacing as distance
darkness erases like chalk,
like dreams she's tunneling through like a mole,
her father neatly tucked out of town on business.

Pulse of the heater beside me dense
as silence I slip into like water, each depth
insisting the mind is clearer than before.

Small pockets of vision rising
like soufflé all the way into morning,
a promise of coffee, my own face
among the opposite plants.

Delicacies

Bears won't come near this honey, defended
every inch of the way by thorns longer than
even the bodies of hornets, thicker
than porcupine quills—these gooseberries your

fingers learn safely to find, exploring
the meaning of once-a-year *delicacy* like
land newly discovered, inherited idiom
grandmothers knew—these

gooseberries must be worth more
than a sweet tooth satisfied. Two
hours at least in the picking—one at
a time, small melons random all over the vine.

Not your compliant blueberries, stripped
by the handful. Not
blackberries so big
you don't need so many or even the silent

bells of salal, lined up mild as lullabies
almost remembered. Gooseberries
two hours more in one-by-one snipping off
blossoms with fingernails, dried

tassels of green
Chinese lanterns. Luminescent. Time
when doing this there's
not much else you can do. Not

laundry. Not dishes. Not changing
diapers or mopping the floor. Time
for more than fingers to be pricked
into remembrance—new

reverence for the unrecorded
delicacy of dreams that must
once have gone on in all of our lives,
uninterrupted, for hours.

Signals

Just in time my sister remembers to put on the baby
the sweater Mother knit her.
It's Christmas, they've driven all day, and the day
before leaving I know (I've done it, myself)
she was running from this store to that,
one last roll of Scotch tape, Pampers, stocking
stuffers, food for the cats who will have to look
out for themselves and the baby as always
wanting to nurse at the worst
possible times. And watching the clock, Mother
already (I know, though I haven't myself arrived
wearing the earrings my sister
last Christmas gave me) is chopping
all the onions for stuffing; the turkey
the freezer has kept for a month, thawing;
the cookies too many to eat, patient under
plastic wrap on the living room table; her fingers
so arthritic each stitch in that sweater she says
is not very good (though really it is,
I couldn't have done it) a penance for lapses
all of us every day make without knowing, balancing
need against need, these signals
we send to each other no words could
in any other possible way bring home.

Dream

1

She's dead, they tell you
she hasn't returned, the boat
was out all night, the waves, the storm
you slept through, how could

you leave her with strangers, not leave word
where you could be reached,
you didn't

give her permission to die without you,
body a leaf, a clump of grass

(*pull in your tongue, it doesn't become you*)

arms peaceful as bells, each side.

2

Alive, you intend
to find her, water around you colder than fear,
grief taking you in like the mother
you should have been

you should know
she wouldn't give up
needing you

to find her
on the sand on the island, watching them
comb their golden mermaid hair

to wrap yourself about her like a shell

tongue the sand from her hair, her cheeks,
her eyes, her white skin smooth as a pulse

to believe your love is stronger than anger.

A Bib for Anne's Daughter

"The days go by and they don't have names."

Jodi Hanauska, fourth grade,
Twin Oaks School

Tonight the freedom, time I'd looked for to celebrate
Rosanna's birth, I thought I knew finally how to
juggle impulse and action, my own daughter
who last week turned ten and all day kept saying
she couldn't believe it, keeping me yet once more
from a poem about her, for Anne, helping me

help her sew this bib of gingham and calico,
rosebud prints and lace for a baby's eating habits
useless as raincoats for waterfalls. Green
elephant applique thick in the trunk, she wants
to do more herself, to stitch perhaps
her fourth or fifth seam, her first real garment,
how long these firsts can go on.

And how I always kept track:
first smile, first tooth, first words that
too soon became too many to write. Tonight
how she mourned her own childhood, "Slipping
away," she cried, "drop by drop,
it's under the sheet now. Slipping down."

This bib for Anne's daughter, still nursing and not
really in need of it ever, her mother
needing time of her own, perhaps this inarticulate
bib in the making—three hours when I
with my daughter knew something here mattered,
grief with love stitched into bone—naming
something no one expects not to last,
too precious not in some way to pass on.

Our Daughter, Thirteen, Says She Is Spending the Night with a Friend

Coming home from the movies, we say this
was the right choice, she wouldn't have
liked it anyway. No

danger. No sex. So wholesome even the dogs
behaved, their tongues at the end of the fifty
mile race discreet, out of sight.

And we enter the silent house more silent
knowing this silence will last all night long,
no sudden explosions of music through air vents,

nerves we didn't know we had
developed like shields, invisible guardians love
demands of the self so that it can keep

on giving, tangible now as moments of change
no one notices: one last bedtime
story we didn't remark upon,

when did we last pick her up? This daughter
who won't read the paper we left this morning
pointedly open, the nine-year-old girl in the next town

two days missing found dead. Daughter
we don't yet know next weekend with friends
will call from a phone booth at midnight,

not say where she is, although later
the ending will turn out all right. Beginning,
each night this watching with nothing to see.

Another Dream

Of course it shouldn't
mean anything

Roller coaster round
and simple as a snail

A simple beginner's track
for a child at grown-up

Height, drawing me into
abandon   a flag

Each time around I wave at her
incredulous   standing

Next to her father
she counts them

Six times
Would you try it

Yourself now
holding my hand

Holding me back from the center
of the circle   a cairn

A sign of stone
on stone

The base of a fountain
dry as fear

Snake in the center issuing
towards us   farther

Than fireworks (Fourth-
of-July small pellets we light

with a match)   it keeps
on coming   harmless

I should be
telling you

Shame , shame   this fear
of a snake

Blossoming
calm as intention towards

A single trillium   flower
your father and I found growing alone

Hiking the base of Sahalie Falls
where later we married

In April the snow at our feet
waxed hard and smooth as

Trillium petals we later
etched into our own silver rings

Three-petalled trillium opening here
like certainty   this

Is the flower
of God.

Déjà Vu

August, before.

This countertop, white
bowl of plums:

two purple
two green

two the small red
throat of the hummingbird.

Still life someone
else in

some other
life could have painted:

this glimpse
not of the past but the future

you, like a blossom too busy
blooming

all along
unknowing, dreamed.

No. 14. Duet

"And in one Lord, Jesus Christ, light of light, very God of God: who for us and for our salvation came down from heaven."

Johann Sebastian Bach
Mass in B Minor

Poised between
idea
and action, one

God and incarnation, this
circular motion could be complete
in itself

eternal as waves
cresting
a spiral:

birds
butterflies
playful

advancing
retreating
        in unum

together
voices revolving
precise as

constellations
around the north star
the point

where all
is possible
nothing

exists without
its opposite
heaven and earth

mind and emotion
lovers
    in unum

knowing beyond
logic the point
between *agape*

and *eros*, reflections
of each in the other, sun
and moon, *lumen*

de lumine, circling
the source of creation
Eve

the reflection of Adam
Adam of God
God of who knows what and we

go on faith, trusting
            Et
               ex Patre

only in sound
in spirit incarnate
a promise of grace

so profoundly delicate we
prolong
our own expectations like

a *pas de deux*
        Deum
            de Deo

voices turning
back
on themselves, restraint

and abandon, who
is the leader
who the led?

Voices
rising, falling
in unison

kites
in the same
wind

dolphins
parallel over
the waves

butterflies stitching
together the breath of the meadow:
a movie you may have seen

where the lovers are fated never
to live
out their lives together

an echo
pagan and Christian
of what could

be, has been,
hands we extend
each to the other

>   *per quem*
>   *omnia*
>   *facta sunt*

the moment of change in
the space between fingertips
Michaelangelo saw

Bach heard
the echoes of old and new
testaments

tangible
>   *descendit*
>   *de coelis*

Botticelli's madonna:
her robe blue as ocean
as sky, wordless

the source of all song
forever visible, over and over
the moment the gift is given.

Reunion

We could go over and over it, why it
didn't work out: white sea
foam in the parking lot
spiraling, such

a winter storm and we
intent on getting the past
straight and out
of the way: corkscrew

breaking just after we'd bought it,
picnic we hadn't prepared for, the rest
of the time we never would have again.
"Look," you said

"feathers for shoulders": foam
I tried to capture on film
pillowing
out of the rocks, the rain

stopping we said just for us
long enough. "That's crazy,"
I said, not meaning it, knowing it
was what anyone could have said

about us, going
just so far and no more: ridge line
trail above us hidden
in trees where years

ago alone in this same
exquisite confusion I dreamed
I would take you, never
dreaming there could be chances to miss.

At the Rancho la Brea Museum, Los Angeles

"However certain our expectations
The moment foreseen may be unexpected
When it arrives."

T.S. Eliot
Murder in the Cathedral

1

There are places the present
gathers itself like a fist and won't
let go.

Choices tug: who knows
what lies ahead.

Layer on layer what could
have been, in the end
the same as what was.

Certainty
deeper than breath.

What could we ever have done
we didn't
at least once try?

2

And we could forever
look back
this way:

Where the saber tooth leaped
on the dire wolf stuck with the stork the whole
lot of them drowned, the stories of

five hundred thousand
in bone still
volunters sift through.

Epics of femur and tibia.
Legends of ribs reconstructed.
Smaller than printers' type, labelled,

divided: truth in the teeth
of mice, the claws of insects: language
before it was born.

3

Now you see her,
now you don't, that skeleton
woman a trick of light
turns whole.

And back once again, relentless
illusion, truth
laid bare with deception.
Layer on layer:

the woman I was
with you, her voice
buried for years
reappearing. This moment

we hadn't expected, resolving
the past: that we would want
to go on, the flesh
was still alive.

4

Dry, it was all on the surface: a crescent
moon shattered like glass
still of a piece: milk agate
centuries, waves bonded smooth.

Looks like something is in it, you said, and right
then it did look deep: a surprise
in the stone. Like the cut one
I'd given you first.

A souvenir impulse polished
beyond what water made natural.
Frozen, a yolk
forever breaking. A sun.

5

This is the way we live now, you say,
as if calling a spade a spade
makes it any less black,

the dirt it could shoulder
more acceptable not
pretending otherwise.

And still I would dig.
I was afraid, I said.
I said I didn't have time.

True, all of them,
none of the good reasons hold.
But this

I couldn't say to your face,
the oldest
one in the world: revenge.

That too.

What I never wanted, you say,
I wanted. Too much.
No other translation.

This open admission you try
not to hear. As though one of us
could in advance have known.

Inflorescence

n. 1. A flowering; flourishing. 2. Bot. a) The mode of
arrangement of flowers in relation to the stem or axis.
b) A cluster of flowers. c) All the flowers growing on a
single plant. d) A single flower.

1

Thunder again southwest unfolding, south-
east, northeast, north like yesterday these
black edges of blossoms centering everywhere, each

Day this celestial inflorescence shadowing
hills, mesas, lavender blue the desert, lavender green,
the names of color flowers better would sing—

Lupine, penstemon, larkspur, sage, here
I'm learning them all: color wheels long ago
all of our seventh-grade class had to make.

Fine gradations of tone, thin grace notes. Test
all of us failed: How many stairs to the classroom?
What color the hall? The teacher

Who taught us to see, sent home
before her own condition was visible, taut
as the canvasses she left behind.

Full as a color wheel, from
that time on centered
we always assumed, at home.

2

"If you love me, you wouldn't have gone," my
daughter convinces herself on the phone. A handle.
Door that won't open, a false room. Something

She hangs onto, knowing I left for only part
of summer, the calendar before I left marked
when I'd be home. Today

She was to have visited.
Rift between us I should have expected, two
continents so far away we can't even rub each other

Wrong: like a storm, the stern
cargo of self-remonstration all of us from childhood back
bear, thinking we've been on our own.

3

Seeing it, isn't the same as being between
doors, open from nothing
to nothing, framed free-standing in air

In a desert unnaturally flat, flat
yellow crumpled, the rug on the sand
the robes of the woman the artist in nineteen

Forty-six put barefoot upon it, the baby
disconsolate echo of her own expression,
capped in ruffles, nursery white:

Tanning's "Maternity" turned away from the sculpture,
unrecognizable, small as genitals on
the horizon, black

Sky bearing down turbulent
as decision where choice
doesn't exist.

4

Below this window the meadow, the young
woman who just this morning I helped sneak
over the gate to sit in the meadow, to sketch

A desert below I have every day
wakened to, rich as a soul on loan and forgotten,
returned: sunlight

Mapping space wider than inspiration, this mountainside,
legends of those here before: the one
who left three children forever, to live with the writer;

The painter whose husband for the sake of her art
chose to have none, to whom
just yesterday I sent a poem. Jenny in

The meadow below me wrapped in flowers
bright as stained glass, the small
ministrations of sun for whom it is only

Beginning—through her hands charcoal
blossoming here in the green
tradition of needles and stars.

Arms small around knees, small talismans
against the sky, the journey this day
interrupted, against all chance of goodbye

How many hours did she sit there alone?
Her solitude I kept returning to look at off-center
the way we see stars, blinded by moon,

That region where words cannot travel
fragile as dreams, the fine alluvium we
bring into all we do.

Her drawing I later found rolled between cedar
slats of the gate: forever the whole
circle I see from this window,

Meadow to mesas to mountains, the clouds
too big for the top edge of paper,
forever right here the center

Opening
outward, balancing this
wild exuberant gesture of sky.

Under a Night Sky

To have walked on the moon and returned
to look back up at it, saying
I've been there, my father

wonders how it must feel to them now:
how nothing—earth, sky—can ever
be the same, themselves

the men their families see perhaps
even tonight
like us, sitting in the back

yard, after
dinner, simply
looking up, one

of our old ways of finding each other after
I grew beyond laps and like an oversized
heart the familiar

Braille of our fingertips failed,
stories becoming
all we knew we could go by: my father

a child surviving
earthquakes in Chile,
the wrath of the plague;

my father the gymnast turned
bank clerk becoming the captain's
steward, proving

himself
hand over hand to the top of the highest
mast, impressing the crew, his daughter

years later who
in his voice saw moonlight
singing

over the backs of dolphins around Cape Horn
where still one hundred
days from land the radio

stopped, the captain
had only the stars
to go by: light

from these same stars we don't
know are still burning or not
next week I'll see from my own

home two thousand miles
away; these distances memory bridges
small as a word and oh so lastingly bright.

III

SINGING THE MOZART REQUIEM

Singing the Mozart Requiem

I

"For who in the World will both mourn
and rejoice at once and for the same reason?"

T.S. Eliot

Some of us already older than Mozart was when death
tipped the job to his student it isn't
your usual courage

> *Quam olim Abrahae*
> *pro-*
> *misisti*

that every week
brings us here
Abraham isn't

first on our minds
promises fail the rest eternal
these words plead for

hopefully many years off
knowing this

> *Et lux perpetua*

is the twentieth century
this

> *Et lux perpetua*

breath we
utter together
is not

going to bring
back the selves we know
we ourselves

have buried the promises
all of us once made never
to grow

old to add
layers of caution like rings on a tree
saying this

rehearsal is re-
creation a justification to families
friends time taken from keeping

up with the news the job what we say

          Dona eis

we owe ourselves this

exhilaration again
unexpected we are
at this moment alive.

II

          "Please, answer. To talk together is
          the only way to survive."

          Wera Küchenmeister
          Letter, East Berlin

Last year where under the vow of silence
for centuries monks
built their stone walls so thick sunlight
still enters surprised
we sang.

No audience   *Hostias*
listened, we sang
for sound itself, a rehearsal—   *et preces*
that choir from Frankfurt out
for a day on the Rhine. Listen,

you never have heard such song.
What stone gave back   *Tibi*
it gave
ten times over: *Domini*
pleas demanding

attention no god
could ignore, no grave
could not be moved by.
Where sunlight knelt down
that song rose.

It was right that the amsel ignored us.
Over our heads she fluted
back and forth with food, her nest
high on the saint's carved crown.
Her chicks filled out rests with their drone.

And it could have seemed that day out of time
the rest of the world was elsewhere: *Quam olim Abrahae*
missiles arriving hours from us
were not waiting burial, peace   *promisisti*
talks were not breaking down,

riding back on the bus thinking next year
the amsel will nest,
this choir will sing somewhere else.
Stones will once again keep their silence.
Sunlight will kneel in grave silence.

This is what I must say I believe.

III

> *"After silence, that which comes next to*
> *expressing the inexpressible is music."*
>
> Aldous Huxley

Three months without sun, his mission
locked in Antarctic ice, my Chilean cousin

survived hearing
Mozart, the only composer he found

really sane, the only to balance
promise and

memory—Requiem
wordless this

region of ice and clouds, Abraham's mountain,
admitting our own

helplessness once
again we begin.

"Puedo escribir los versos mas tristes esta noche,"
my cousin quoted Neruda

driving to mining camps, fishing towns, children
not knowing sacrifice by not

knowing anything
else, the name

"Allende"
red on walls around schools, banks, private

gardens hidden below
jagged glass set in cement.

IV

Yes, I can be tempted and some
days I say

All right, art is not
after all moral, this Requiem

as we sing it has nothing to do with the world
we in our distances try

to imagine: threat
in the hands of Victor Jara

voice of García Lorca still
Chile and Spain remember: as though

silence were not
also loudly political and this Requiem

no common eulogy
in this time

in this twentieth century
this inexorable push to a common extinction

the tests of courage placed
on us

the tests we place on ourselves.

V

As far beyond definition as beauty,
beauty profound as grief

these are not words we use easily,
shields for defense, these melodies circling
towards a moment where every

note
balances time
and our knowledge of time

Benedictus

my father
eighty, for whom each day is a blessing
my mother
already surviving all those back home

Benedictus

the child
I was I can only begin to remember
not needing ever
to know what it is we should live for

Qui venit

this autumn without
rain each
day a few more leaves

Lux aeterna

turning until
every tree in town celebrates
sunlight we hardly feel we deserve

Requiem

holding our breath

each leaf on each tree poised for the least
wind.

NOTES

Pilgrim Pumpkin

*"Aquí mismito te dejo
 hecho un copihue mi corazón"*

> The moment I leave you, my heart will turn into a *copihue* (bell-shaped, scarlet blossom, the national flower of Chile); from the folk song "Chile Lindo"

"my small college sent to bear goodwill"

> The time is 1963. The college is Cornell College, Iowa—which was participating in a student exchange program called The Experiment in International Living.

*"Lo mismo cómo hacemos
 en los Estados Unidos"*

> The same as we do in the United States

"All / Saints' Day mass pilgrimage"

> Hallowe'en is not celebrated in Chile, but November 1 is a national holiday devoted to decorating family graves.

Singing the Mozart Requiem

I

"Some of us already older than Mozart was when death
 tipped the job to his student"

> Mozart was in the process of composing the Requiem, a funeral mass, when he died at age 35. One of his students, Xaver Süssmayr, completed it from sketches Mozart had left.

"Quam olim Abrahae promisisti"

> Which thou didst promise of old to Abraham (from the Offertorium)

"Et lux perpetua"

> And perpetual light (from the Introit)

"Dona eis"

> Give to them (from the Introit)

II

The setting of this section is Kloster Eberbach, an eleventh-century monastery in West Germany.

"Hostias et preces, Tibi Domini"

Sacrifice and prayer unto Thee, O Lord (from the Offertorium)

"amsel"

blackbird

"missiles arriving hours from us"

Summer of 1983. U.S. Pershing missiles were being shipped to West Germany for installation.

III

The setting of this section is Chile, 1963, before President Salvador Allende was elected to office. My cousin, a dentist who had traveled with the Chilean Navy to Antarctica, was showing me the countryside.

"Puedo escribir los versos mas tristes esta noche."

I could write the saddest poems tonight.

IV

"Victor Jara"

One of Chile's most popular poets and folk singers. In September 1973, in Santiago, he and 6,000 others, mainly university students, were held prisoner for three days by the military, who were engaged in overthrowing the constitutional government of Socialist President Salvador Allende. Large numbers of students were killed. Jara's fingers were chopped off with an axe, and he was then machine-gunned to death.

"García Lorca"

Federico García Lorca, one of Spain's most prominent poets, disappeared and was later found murdered during the Spanish Civil War, in 1936. He was 37.

V

"Benedictus, Qui venit"

>Blessed is he who comes (from the Benedictus)

"Lux aeterna"

>Eternal light (from Agnus Dei)

"Requiem"

>Rest (from Agnus Dei)